GEORGE SHRINKS

GEORGE SHRINKS

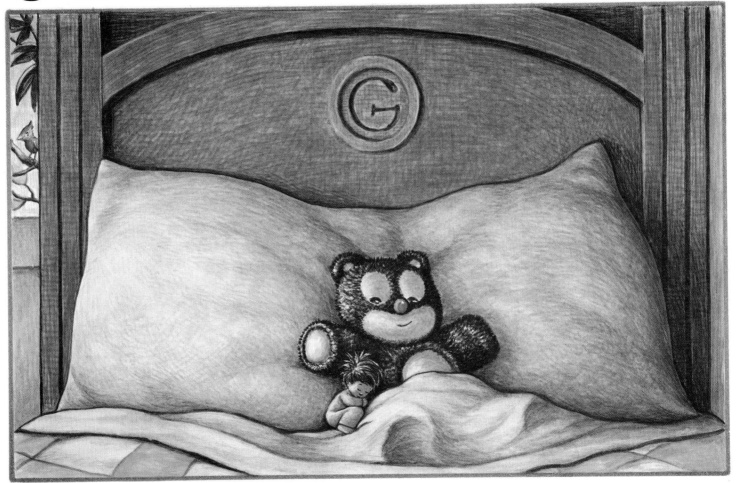

STORY AND PICTURES BY WILLIAM JOYCE

SCHOLASTIC INC.
NEW YORK TORONTO LONDON AUCKLAND SYDNEY

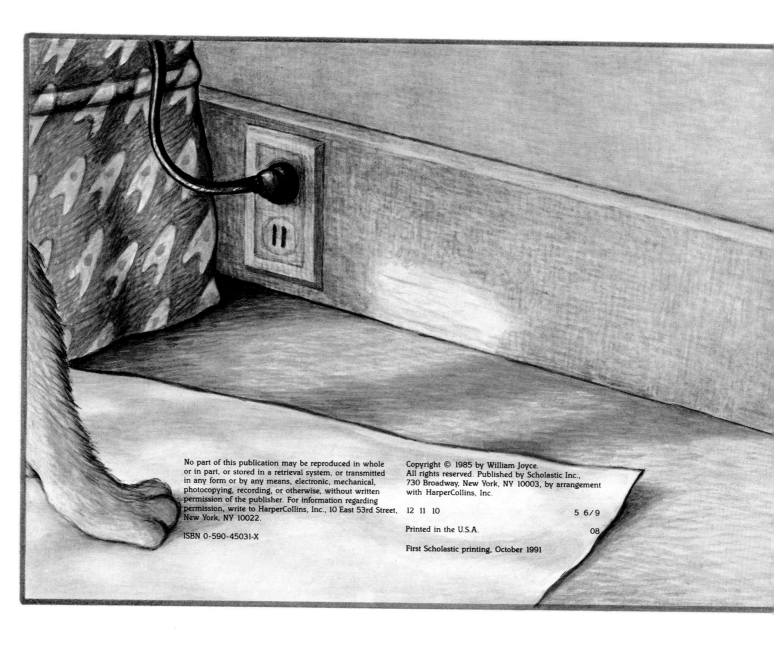

Copyright © 1985 by William Joyce.
All rights reserved. Published by Scholastic Inc.,
730 Broadway, New York, NY 10003, by arrangement
with HarperCollins, Inc.

12 11 10   5 6/9

Printed in the U.S.A.   08

First Scholastic printing, October 1991

One day, while his mother and father were out,
George dreamt he was small,
and when he woke up he found it was true.

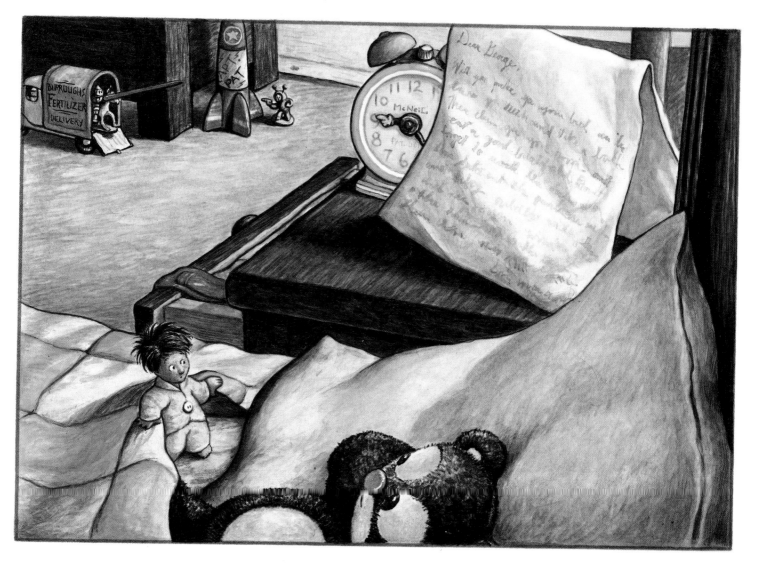

His parents had left him a note:

"Dear George," it said. "When you wake up,

please make your bed,

brush your teeth,

and take a bath.

Then clean up your room

and go get your little brother.

Eat a good breakfast,

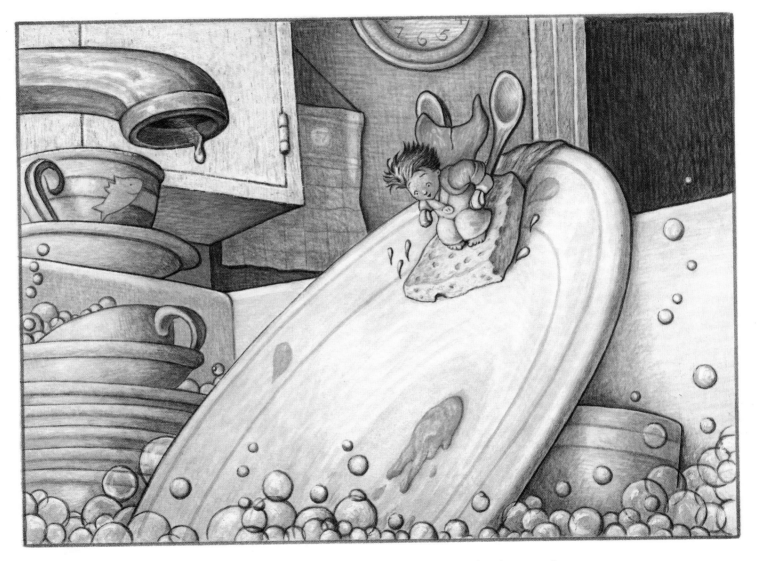

and don't forget to wash the dishes, dear.

Take out the garbage,

and play quietly.

Make sure you water the plants

and feed the fish.

Then check the mail

and get some fresh air.

Try to stay out of trouble,

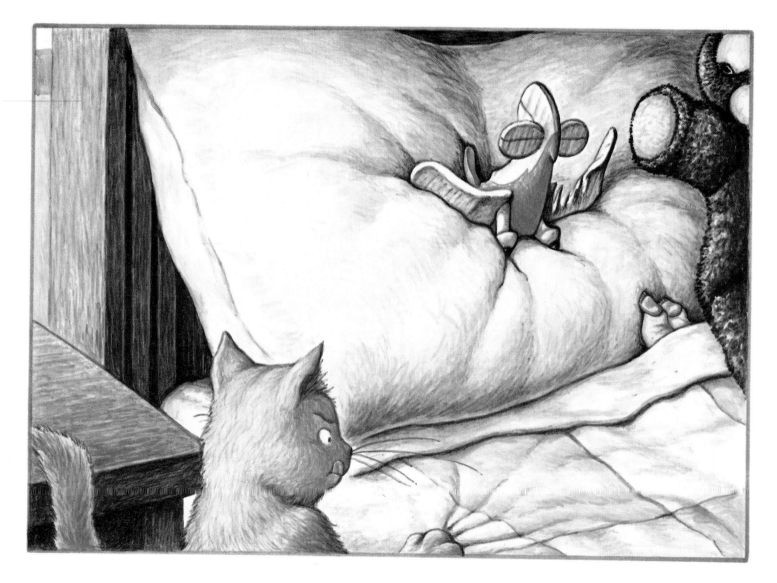

and we'll be home soon.

Love, Mom and Dad.''